Ira Nelson Morris

With the Trade-Winds

a jaunt in Venezuela and the West Indies

Ira Nelson Morris

With the Trade-Winds
a jaunt in Venezuela and the West Indies

ISBN/EAN: 9783337316037

Printed in Europe, USA, Canada, Australia, Japan

Cover: Foto ©Andreas Hilbeck / pixelio.de

More available books at **www.hansebooks.com**

AUTHOR IN INTERIOR TRAVELLING COSTUME,
VENEZUELA.

Frontispiece.

With the Trade-Winds

A Jaunt in Venezuela and the West Indies

By

IRA NELSON MORRIS

(Second Edition)

" The benefit of travel comes not from the distance
traversed, nor from the scenes reflected on the retina,
but from the intellectual stimulus thus awakened,
and the amount of thought and reading which results therefrom. . . . Expansion, growth, broader
experience and wider charity, these are the fruits of
that real travel which is of the mind."

J. L. STODDARD

G. P. PUTNAM'S SONS
New York and London
1897

PREFATORY

THE desire to impart to my readers some elementary knowledge of a South American region of which but little has ever been written in the English tongue, has led to this small volume. It gives a desultory account of what I saw and heard, together with personal experiences during a recent winter tour among the West India Islands and in Venezuela.

I wish to express my grateful thanks to my kind friend, the Marquis Montelo, whose companionship contributed so much to fill the tour with profitable knowledge as well as with interest and pleasure.

IRA NELSON MORRIS.

CHICAGO, 1896.

CONTENTS

PAGE

ILLUSTRATIONS

ix

WITH THE TRADE-WINDS

I.

OUTWARD BOUND

ON a very cold day in December I stood on the deck of the steamer *Madiana* as she slowly pushed her way through the ice toward the Narrows below New York.

After leaving the luxurious Waldorf to face the biting cold winds and accommodate one's self to the surroundings which the steamer affords, I must say I did not wonder at my friends asking how I could choose to take such an out-of-the-way sort of trip. Not that the *Madiana* is an uncomfortable boat, for that would be doing it an injustice, but I anticipated a second *Majestic* or *Teutonic*, and in this I was disappointed.

At half-past five the familiar gong one hears on shipboard announced dinner. My place was at the right of our good captain, Mr. Fraser. Next to me sat Mr. Maynard, of New York, while opposite sat Count Bismarck, of Germany, one of the younger generation of that celebrated name. It was not long before the captain and the gentleman whom hereafter I shall call our friend Maynard began a conversation which at once showed how well both were acquainted with the places we were leaving home comforts to visit, and how much profit might be derived from their companionship.

Our captain, a short, stout fellow, was the typical sea-dog. His appearance would answer to the description of the hero in almost any sea-faring romance. It was now Friday, and he informed us it would be Tuesday evening of the next week before we should reach St. Thomas, our first stopping-place, and

only one island of twelve that we were
going to visit on our way to Venezuela,
before the boat would again turn toward
the cold north.

At first some of the ladies looked a
little "home-sick," but as time ad-
vanced the salon assumed a cheerful
aspect, and we began to notice our
companions for the next few weeks.
Acquaintance is soon made at sea ; and
by the fourth day out, partly through
good jokes, but mainly through our
amiable captain, everybody knew everybody, and the best of fellowship pre-
vailed. About the third day people
began discarding their winter garments,
and on the fourth I strolled about in
tennis flannels and a straw hat.

One evening after dinner, as I walked
the deck in a dreamy mood, thinking of
the far-away countries I was about to
visit, I observed a charming girl of about
twenty seated comfortably on a steamer
lounge ; this fair maiden, with the

moon's soft rays about her, added new
lustre to the surroundings. The smoke
from my pipe circled in graceful wreaths,
drawing me into a state of reminis-
cence, and soon my thoughts wandered into strange lands, carrying with
them fanciful pictures of what a southward trip might be in the company of
one so gracious, who should share my
travels and my experiences. Such were
my first dreams in the tropics ; and a
few nights later I was happy to find
them not evanescent, like the smoke
from my pipe, and blown away forever,
but reappearing in all their beauty in
actual life.

II.

THE Tropics breed romance. Something in the air seems to stimulate one to adventure and awaken that spirit of sentiment which burns dimly in all of us.

Imagine coasting the luxuriant islands of the Indies with a mellow moon to cast the shadows of another world across your mind and to awaken the fondest dreams of youth into reality It was on such a night as this that we sat on the aft deck telling stories of adventure. All were listening to a bit of the early life and struggles of the Indies, which the captain related somewhat as follows :

5

" From the time when Columbus first landed on Salvador, and the wealth and beauty of the islands were reported abroad, it was not very long before other adventurous Europeans discovered many other islands in the neighborhood, equally beautiful and even larger than that which Columbus found. Some of the expeditions sent over from Europe were for military glory and the gain of new territory ; some were parties arrayed by rich and venturesome nobles in England, France, and other countries. It was by means of these expeditions that the great groups of islands known to us as the Indies fell into the hands of European nations.

" Not to say," continued the captain, " that you are to understand each expedition coming over had only to plant a flag and the island was theirs ; no, indeed ! They first had to fight and conquer the native Indians or Caribs. Then they were constantly fighting

among themselves as to who first discovered the place and whether it should
belong to France, Spain, England, or
some other country that was sending
out expeditions at the time.

" It was no easy matter to take away
the islands from the Indians. The
Caribs were a powerful people, supposed
to have crossed over from South America. The conquest of a people like this
on their own territory and knowing
every inch of the ground was no easy
task.

" Many are the cruel stories told of
fights and hardships endured by these
gentlemen, who left their native homes
in search of gold and glory.

" Well, as now I hear the coxswain
strike four bells, I must go and prepare
for an early rise, for by to-morrow evening if all is smooth sailing, I mean to
drop anchor in St. Thomas, our first
stopping-place."

I did not care to follow the example

of the rest of the party by saying good-night, but arm in arm with my fair companion, whom I met in a very romantic way,—as my dream itself had indicated—we strolled the deck until the night-watch was relieved, for it was one of those beautiful nights on the sea when the faint silvery bell struck by the sailor on the bridge expresses no idea as regards time. Surrounded by such scenes and amid such circumstances time is measured only by one's impulses and emotions.

CHARLOTTE AMALIA, CAPITAL OF ST. THOMAS.

III.

IT was growing dark. One by one the silver stars peeped out of the blue firmament, and the great moon silently cast her silver rays upon the dark waters. In the quiet and peace of this summer night there stretched before us the beautiful harbor of the small Danish island of St. Thomas.

Off in the background, reaching half way up the mountain side, like millions of fireflies, rested the capital and only city, Charlotte Amalia.

On entering the bay we noticed a German man-of-war at anchor, quietly riding the waves. A little farther on we saw two French cruisers and a Span-

9

ish gunboat.   These men-of-war, representing the great nations of the world,
seemed to add importance to the island,
and we were told that prior to the last
twenty years, before Barbadoes rose into
such popularity, this small island of
Denmark's was the chief coaling station
and outfitting place for those boats of
the world which found themselves in
need in Southern waters.

A few more turns of the screw and
we were anchored about a mile away
from a sort of pier running into the
water.   Leaning over the rail of the
Madiana I beheld a scene of commotion
and excitement.   About a hundred small
rough boats manned by strong negroes
of the island were crowding around the
hull of our great boat, looking as though
any moment they might be crushed like
egg-shells.   This being a regular occur-
rence at each port we visited, and as it
was a striking feature of the trip, I
shall describe our experience with these
fellows.

These negroes are wonderfully well
built ; it is a pity that they so shun
work. Labor, except what is an abso-
lute necessity, is, in their eyes, useless
and degrading. Many of them gain
their only living by owning a clumsy
boat similar to the many which I have
described around our steamer. With
these they carry passengers to and from
the shore when a steamer is in harbor,
and during the many other days they
are engaged in unloading and carrying
freight from sailing vessels and other
freight boats. Their cries and shouts
to passengers on the steamer, persuad-
ing the latter to take boat to shore, are
much worse than any with which I have
ever been besieged by the army of cab-
men at the Grand Central Station in
New York. The sight of these fellows
fighting and pushing one another about
in their boats, made one think what a
fine foot-ball team they would make to
oppose our Yale eleven.

Col. Maynard and I did not take dinner aboard ship, preferring a stroll on land, and a visit to one of the hotels, situated on high cliffs overlooking the sea. On arriving ashore we seemed to amuse the negroes in a high degree. These simple-minded people are indeed very easily amused, but let me remark that there is this difference between the negro of the West Indies and his brother of the States : the former has learned that his position is not like that of the educated white man, therefore he does not presume to place himself on the same footing.

It is needless to say how much we enjoyed our first dinner in the Indies. Not alone was the food delicious, but it was a rare pleasure to sit on an open verandah overlooking the sea, while behind us rose the great volcanic mountains.

After dinner we " did " the town. One can usually gain an adequate idea of a town in one of these islands by walking

down the main business street and observing the people, the shops, and the
houses. The negroes are always jolly
and laughing : this is the only side of
life they know : if they have sufficient
food for mere existence they are satisfied. In these hot climates clothing is
dispensable.

The houses and shops are for the
most part built in one story, and are
constructed chiefly of a soft native
stone. The poorest houses are framed
by poles and then covered over with
palm leaves stuck together with mud,
which quickly hardens in this hot climate.

The few foreign residents, who form
the representative and best element in
all the Islands, have their homes on the
outskirts of the town, or back among
the hills, where they enjoy the breeze
of the trade-winds and a cleanliness not
to be found in the towns themselves.

In the general market-place loud-voiced negroes, both men and women, offered their vegetables and wares for sale. The fruits which grow so luxuriantly on the Islands are most tempting, even though handled by the dusky maid of Africa.

Some of the large stores and warehouses in the town are kept by foreigners who, anxious for the advantage of trade, endure the hot climate of the island. In the shops one can find most articles of manufacture from both the United States and Europe.

We spent two days in St. Thomas, driving about the island, and seeing many queer things.

Just as the twilight fell we were again rowed to the *Madiana*. All was quiet save for the plaintive voices of the negroes singing on the shore, which the wind wafted to us across the water. With the melody echoing in the distance we drifted out to the open sea on our way to Santa Cruz.

IV.

A NIGHT OF ROMANCE IN THE INDIES

" HAVE you a guitar?" whispered my fair companion as we mounted the steps from the salon.

Our boat was dreamily skirting the shore of the beautiful island of Tortola. The silver rays of the moon reflected on the waters below a miniature of mountains clothed in rich tropical verdure.

There was nothing to mar the quiet of the scene. The rippling waves played a soft accompaniment to the sweet voice of my friend. We were lazily reclining on some rugs in the stern of the boat. Lulled by the sweet voice of my companion, and the faint murmuring of the guitar, I felt that I must invent a story for the occasion—one full of romance and adventure.

I related how during the last century, while England and Spain were engaged in bitter war, a sweet and noble girl of Devonshire was kidnapped by some Spanish brigands after a severe fight in the village. She was taken aboard ship with other captives to be borne to the West Indies to serve as slaves or be treated as heretics in some miserable monastery. Among those engaged in the affray and left seriously wounded was the lover of this girl,—a handsome, manly fellow, about twenty-eight years old. Though thinking himself about to die, the hero made an oath that if he should by any possibility survive, he would avenge himself on those who had wrecked his happiness, and spend the rest of his days in seeking her who was dearest on earth to him, thus proving that honor is the foundation of an Englishman's code.

Perched on the high cliffs whose rocks are washed by the blue sea, rests the Spanish monastery of Santa Juanita. The silver bell pealed forth the hour of midnight. Before the altar in prayer knelt a woman whose thoughts were bent on her home in Devonshire, far across the sea.

Half a league from the island, quietly riding the waves, rocked the ship of some English buccaneers on whose deck, if the moon were bright enough, could be observed armed men preparing for a land attack. Impatiently pacing the deck, clad in a military cloak, with sabre and pistols, was a young officer— no other, indeed, than the hero of the brigand fight in the small seaport town of Devonshire.

The boat carried no lights : all was quiet as death. The plan of action which the party adopted was to gain the shore, quickly surprise the Spanish guards, take the town and capture the

2

monastery, reported to contain fabulous wealth, and—above all—some English souls.

But things did not turn out so fortunately. The Spanish soldiers, hidden by thick underbrush on shore, quietly awaited their victims, and the handful of brave English fellows were soon overpowered. Many were killed, and in the quiet and peace of the night the Spaniards dragged the wounded to the cloister to be cared for by the Sisters.

The woman who knelt at prayer earlier in the evening was now stooping over a dying man. The faint rays of a quaint lamp burning before a shrine cast a dim shadow on the stony floor. The melancholy tones of the old bell came like rays of hope to the ears of an English soldier dying for the love and honor of his sweetheart.

Having brought my story to a close, I awoke from my dreams. My friend was playing a soft plaintive air : from off in the distance, like a far-away echo, came the deep voice of the sailor on lookout, " Twelve o'clock, and all 's well."

V.

SANTA CRUZ, AN ISLAND OF PLANTATIONS

I REACHED deck the next morning just as the sun poised itself over the distant hills. Santa Cruz, like St. Thomas, belongs to Denmark. It is not, however, so mountainous, and the people find more opportunity here for agriculture than on the other island. The town itself is small, and much the same in general character as Charlotte Amalia.

I had accepted an invitation from Mr. Maynard to visit a large sugar plantation in which he is interested. After a light breakfast, we were rowed ashore to the company's office. There we met Col. Blackwood, who is interested in the

A PLANTATION HOUSE, SANTA CRUZ.

estates on the island. We were soon
being driven by a swift team of West
Indian ponies over smooth hard roads
toward the plantation. The country
through which we passed was well-
cultivated.

After travelling some hours between
rows of stately palms and through a
rich country, we noticed in the distance
a mansion of the old colonial days built
imposingly on a great hill. Towards
this we made our way. Here was the
headquarters of the estate.

In better days when West Indian
sugar was a more profitable article and
before the sugar bounty on the continent was known, there existed many
other rich plantations similar to this,
both here and on the other islands. But
in recent times affairs are in a sad state
in all the Indies. This is due primarily
to the decrease in value of sugar, which
is the article of most importance in the
islands. Since the fall of the sugar in-

dustry, the people find it hard to obtain a means of subsistence. Small wonder that most of the old European families of high birth have within the last century drifted away from this region, and that now there remain only the fast decaying estates, with their mansions, to testify of once glorious times. It is a touching sight.

We lunched at the estate, where I met Mrs. Blackwood and her niece, both from Boston. It is charming to experience the true hospitality which the people of these lands always seem so happy to extend to strangers on their shore. Charles Kingsley spoke the truth when he said that the West Indian hospitality and politeness are traits which the people of the continent might well imitate.

The luncheon itself was a typical one. It consisted of fruit of all kinds, including mangoes, plantains, bread-fruit, guavas, and other varieties which I had not seen since my journey a few years

before through Mexico, and also of
several delicious Indian foods of a light
and dainty character.

After luncheon we visited the sugar
factory. This great article of commerce appears to a stranger to be made
in a very simple and easy manner, while
only by one who understands the trade
and the principles of sugar, can the
truly intricate and difficult character of
the process be realized.

In a few words, the sugar-cane is
brought in great carts to the factory,
where it is crushed between gigantic
rollers. The juice thus obtained runs
into great vats, where it stands for clar-
ifying. It is then treated with steam to
a degree of ripeness, and afterwards
allowed slowly to crystallize. These
crystals form the brown sugar, which is
sent in great cakes to the market, usually
the United States, for refining. That
which does not crystallize becomes what
we know as crude molasses, and is

again put through the same process as the juice from the sugar ; that which still remains passes into stills for the manufacture of rum.

Of rum, also a very important article of trade in the Indies, it is needless to say that in former times, when this liquor was more popular, the West Indian was known to be the best.

After a very interesting hour spent at the factory we returned to the house, where we spent the rest of the day on the cool verandas. After dinner, which our excellent hostess presided over in a charming manner, we strolled about the parks under the great trees. But it was now growing late, and as the moon had already risen some hours, we were obliged to bid our kind friends farewell.

There is a peculiar pathos in the parting from such brief acquaintances who have been very kind to us and whom perhaps we shall never see again. That night, as we drove back to the coast, threading our way through great forests, the moon throwing dark shadows across our path, I was unusually sensitive to emotion.

VI.

A FIELD-DAY IN ST. KITT'S

THE next morning I was awakened from my slumbers by the roar of a cannon, followed by other reports whose echoes were driven back by the great mountains rising from the water's edge.

As everything so far had been quiet and peaceful during our voyage, and as in these dreamy lands I had no anticipations pertaining to war of any sort, I was naturally somewhat startled.

Thrusting my head out the port-hole, I noted a few leagues from us several men-of-war at anchor. A little time afterwards I went on deck, just as the *reveille* was wafted within our hearing

from an English man-of-war to our
starboard, and with my glass was able
to observe on the English boats the
sailors taking their muskets and preparing for early morning inspection and
drill.

Count Bismarck had asked me to go
aboard the warship *Blake* for breakfast,
having letters to the captain, whom he
expected to meet in these waters. As
we rowed alongside the ironclad, the
mouths of the great cannon looked
grimly towards us, in sharp contrast
with the very cordial reception we received after boarding the English ves-
sel. Our cards were carried to the
officer of the deck, who at once directed
them to be sent to the captain.

It had always been one of my great
pleasures to make acquaintance with
the captains of vessels. Something
about their very sea-faring life breeds a
frank politeness giving them the qualities of the true gentleman, although

often somewhat hidden under a cloak
of brusque sea manners.

We were fortunate enough to see the
marines drawn up in line for drill, and
interested at the manner in which they
did justice to their colors.

It is hard to realize that one of these
ships is almost a city in itself. Each
man has his own little home and his
daily duties. There is a market-place
where are stored foods of all kinds, and
adjacent to this the place where live-
stock is kept for consumption. Farther
down the gangway we found in the work-
shop men busily engaged in the manufacturing of new implements and the
repairing of the old.

We also saw the tailor-shop and linen
outfit, where clothes were in process of
making and old ones being mended.
Here also was the boot and shoe repairing shop. A blue and white sign at-
tracted our attention to the barber-
shop. In coming back by another

street we passed through the great
kitchen of the cruiser, where food is
cooked for the small city, and the hospital where the sick are kept.

We spent a good part of the morning
aboard the *Blake* ; nor could we make
a graceful retreat without accepting an
invitation from the captain for dinner,
to be followed by a military ball on
deck, given in honor of the governor.

Programmes were distributed about
the *Madiana*, telling us there were to be
athletic games given by the officers and
sailors of the British squadron on the
grounds in Basseterre, the principal
town of the island, off which we were
anchored.

During noon-time we wandered about
the streets visiting all the places of interest to strangers. This was the first
English island we had yet touched on
our voyage, and it surprised us to find
how typically English everything was.
However tropical the surroundings

might be, yet we found everywhere the well-equipped, neat English house, with its tennis-court and cricket set on the lawn.

In the afternoon we noticed happy people at their five o'clock teas or engaging in athletic games, just as at Southampton and Brighton. To be sure, only a very small per cent. of the inhabitants are English, but wherever an Englishman wanders he brings with him his own ideas, customs, and mannerisms. To me the English nation appears not only one of great enterprise, but ranks first as a people that civilized the world.

Pleasant fountains shaded by graceful palms or mangoes, marked the intersection of many of the streets, and numerous little parks were scattered here and there throughout the city. The streets were well-paved and clean ; and the houses, though small, have a neat and sanitary appearance.

About four o'clock we turned our

CAVALRY IN ST. KITT'S.

steps in the direction of the athletic
games.

While these games are not different
in themselves from the ordinary tourna-
ments of athletics that we have in America, there is here added to them the
romantic interest of being given by marines and officers of far-away England.
In the background loom up the great
mountains ; before us, beyond gently
sloping meadows and plains, the ocean
rolls in the distance.

The field was lined with carriages
and vehicles of all kinds, filled with
pretty girls arrayed in striking costumes
for this gala occasion of the week.

Here, through some English folk to
whom I had cards of introduction, I
made some very pleasant acquaintances.

We sat in one of the carriages with a
bevy of fair English ladies, and amidst
the shouts and laughter and confusion
of the throng, thoroughly enjoyed our-

selves.   Popcorn, peanuts, lemonade, sandwiches, soda and the like were all in good form, and to say that we spent a pleasant afternoon would hardly do justice to our appreciation.

VII.

ENSEMBLE

THE Marine Band is playing a dreamy southern air. We are aboard the English warship *Blake*. In the distance, glistening in the moon, the palms sigh. Imagine the romance of a military ball in the tropics !

We were anchored only a short distance from Her Majesty's island of St. Kitt's. The mountains rise from the bosom of the ocean clad in a mantle of rich tropical vegetation.

"Ah ! Count," I say, as the moon appearing from a cloud brings this grand panorama to view, "if there is any spark of true life in a man, this would surely kindle it into nobility ! "

3   33

Thereupon my friend answers, "Why ponder upon such serious thoughts when your friend, yonder pretty American girl, awaits you for this waltz?"

I am soon gliding away in the dance with one of the sweetest girls. We are on the British West India ship, whose deck, garnished by pretty women and handsome officers in full military dress, presents a scene not likely to be forgotten. I am very proud, for well I know my fair friend is the chief attraction of those brave English eyes.

What a night! Shall I ever forget it? Threading our way among the dancers we at last find ourselves in the bow of this mighty ship, under two great cannon (England's pride). Neither of us speak. We thus sit musing some time, till, faintly wafted by the gentle breeze, the peal of the old cathedral bell comes to us. In such times people find in one another that which is most pleasing on earth—feelings in com-

mon ; and these, when based upon
character and the more noble qualities
of man, indeed bring one a little nearer
to true friendship.

VIII.

ANTIGUA—AN OUTING IN THE MOUNTAINS

A FEW hours after returning from the ball, we weighed anchor, and the engines of our boat throbbed once more as we headed again southward on our way to new lands.

Needless to say, I slept the sleep of the happy, and never waked in a more contented mood than I did the next morning. Our graceful ship is on her way towards a dark shadow in the distance, which the captain tells us is Antigua.

It was towards noon when we reached the harbor and our boat once more came to anchor. We were to spend the rest of Saturday and Sunday in Antigua.

IN THE MARKET-PLACE, ST. JOHNS, ANTIGUA.

Next morning Mr. Austin, a young
Englishman with whom I had become
quite intimate, and I, decided to take a
forty-five mile drive around the island.
The road passed through dense forests
and jungles, where there was hardly
enough light at mid-day to read a newspaper ; then again climbed the mountain side or lay along the smooth sandy
beach of the seashore.   On the way we
saw the city reservoir built by the colonial inhabitants.   Here were great piles
of masonry in which much skill in civil
engineering was displayed.   I noticed
on steel plates the names of English
constructionists and engineers.   From
this point, which is situated some twelve
miles distant in the mountains, run a
system of pipes to the city, by which
cool refreshing water of the very best
kind, derived from the mountain springs
and streams, is always obtainable.

Towards evening, as we were still
some distance from the town, we saw a

neat white church situated at the side
of the mountain, from which came
strains of sweet music. We looked at
one another without saying a word, tied
our horses to a tree, entered and took
a seat in the midst of the little negro
congregation. I was particularly impressed by the sincerity of devotion
with which these people worshipped ; I
learned there to respect the negro more
than I had ever before thought it possible
for me to do.

IX

MARTINIQUE, A FRENCH MINIATURE IN THE TROPICS

IF a great searchlight could be levelled at Martinique, it would unfold to the observer a vivid picture like that of gay Paris. Although the rays of life are somewhat diminished in coming such a distance as from France to the West Indies, nevertheless their nature is the same.

Strolling up from the quays whither we had rowed in small boats, we were at once amused and interested. A smile appeared simultaneously on the faces of all of us, the sign on a large yellow placard struck our gaze, announcing that a grand ballet was to be

enacted by the famous X—— of Paris
that evening, followed by a French ball.
We had hardly anticipated such amusement in these romantic lands of the
South.

As we went about some of our party
attempted to exercise their knowledge
of the French tongue, although without
much success in understanding or in
being understood, for the reason that
these people have not a pure speech
but a mixture of French and negro
patois, similar to the " Gumbo " dialect
of New Orleans, which is quite incom-
prehensible to ordinary ears.

The striking feature of St. Pierre,
the largest and principal city of Martinique, is, as I have said, its distinctively French associations. Were it
not for an occasional orange tree, or
some other tropical plant, we could
easily imagine ourselves in one of the
smaller towns of France. Here one
reads French names above the shops,

and finds at the intersections of the streets an occasional statue erected to the memory of some noted Frenchman.

The island of Martinique being very mountainous, the city should have the very best of sanitary equipments, yet what we consider the necessary conditions for health are quite unknown there. The gutters, supplied with fresh and cold water from the streams of the mountains, rush down the sides of the streets, and were it not for these the death-rate at Martinique would be still greater than it now is.

The architecture of the houses is decidedly European, though tending rather towards the light and dainty order than the solid and substantial, representing, like many French people, beauty while it lasts, but quick decay.

In St. Pierre are pretty parks with an occasional murmuring fountain ; also here and there a marble or bronze statue hid by thick foliage. In the quiet of

the evenings hither come the beautiful
French Creoles ; and many a pretty little romance takes place here, ushered
in by a guitar serenade.

One statue brings back reminiscences
of the older days of the French empire.
It represents the patient Josephine,
Empress of the French. Martinique
is her birthplace, and here the simple,
beautiful Creole lived her younger days
and received her first education.

But we could not linger too long
about these pleasant spots, for we had
engaged a *voiture* to drive us to the
botanical gardens and thence to a little
town situated some distance from St.
Pierre, high up in the mountains.

The botanical gardens of Martinique
are known all over the world. Aside
from those of Trinidad they are considered the finest in existence. Taking
into consideration the nature and adap-
tation of the surroundings, I consider
the gardens of Martinique even grander,
as a whole, than those of Trinidad.

A FRENCH CREOLE, MARTINIQUE.

To attempt to describe our walks through the old parks would be a failure, for I could not do justice to the sentiments which were aroused in me on beholding growing in their natural simplicity, side by side, the orange, citron, fig, guava, and many other fruits, in great luxuriance. Bamboo grows here in profusion ; also wild and dainty orchids of all kinds clinging to the rocks and the bark of the trees.

Added to these wonders of growing nature, were great cataracts leaping from the near mountains. All this beauty and grandeur was sufficient to inspire the soul of any man.

After returning to our hotel and resting, we enjoyed an excellent dinner prepared in good style by a French *chef*. Even to the fact of wine appearing on the table free of charge, everything showed the customs of the French transplanted to the island.

Later on in the evening, we found our way through gayly lighted streets,

which appeared like a diminished re-
flection of the Rue de Rivoli, to the
Opera House, where, as previously re-
marked, we had observed a notice to
the effect that a ballet and masked ball
would take place that night.   The ballet
was good ; the French ballet is always
good, comparatively speaking.   The
energy and spirit with which this people
enter into everything is too well known
to comment upon.   The ball, I shall
leave to my readers' imagination ; suffice
it to say that it was similar to any mid-
winter masked ball given at the Madi-
son Square in New York City.

X.

ST. LUCIA, A FORMER GIBRALTAR OF THE WEST INDIES

NO other small island in the West Indies has been the scene of more contention between European powers than St. Lucia.

Speaking of the striking appearance of this rough, volcanic island, and of its convenient situation for military purposes, a recent writer adds : "What wonder that two mighty nations contended for the possession of St. Lucia, as the Greeks and Trojans waged war for the guardianship of fair Helen of old ?"

In 1605 the first attempt was made at colonization, when the English ship

Olive Blossom landed some sixty colonists, who planted the flag of St. George and occupied the island in the name of England. From this time until the capitulation of the French at Fort Morne Fortune, in 1803, there was an almost ceaseless strife for the sovereignty of the island. The following extract, taken from a letter written by Admiral Rodney in 1772 to the Earl of Sandwich, shows the importance with which St. Lucia was regarded : " I had lately the honor to present to your Lordship a copy of a letter I thought it my duty to send to the King's Minister . . . pointing out the great consequence of retaining some of the conquered islands, particularly Martinique or St. Lucia ; and though at that time I preferred the retention of Martinique, I am now fully convinced that St. Lucia is of more consequence to Britain . . . Either of these islands in the hands of Great

Britain must, while she remains a great maritime power, make her sovereign of the West Indies."

Such is a very brief outline of some of the past events. To-day there remain but the fast crumbling forts and barracks as a testimony to this once important military strong-hold.

The old mountain barracks are far more healthful than if along the coast ; the matter of climate being one of the most important things England has to study in choosing her tropical locations. Thus at Aden on the Red Sea, reported to be one of the hottest places on the globe, it is necessary for the Government to relieve the soldiers every few months by sending fresh recruits thither from other tropical countries where they have been accustomed to serve.

Great dredging machines, similar to those used in Panama, were sent over to deepen the waters of the harbor, so that now steamers of the largest draught can land immediately at the side of the pier. This is something unknown to almost all the Islands and harbors of South America.

St. Lucia has also been made one of the coaling stations of England. It was with great interest that I watched a large German merchant steamer being coaled in this remote section of the world. The manner in which they coal these boats is unique. From 75 to 150 negroes, both men and women, are supplied with rough baskets of one or two bushels capacity, which they are compelled to carry on their heads. It is very hard work, and on inquiry I ascertained that these poor wretches are only paid at the rate of a few cents an hour.

St. Lucia seemed to me one of the loveliest of the West India islands. While I was sitting here on deck one evening, our boat being fastened alongside the pier, familiar airs of religious music were wafted thither by the breeze. On inquiry I learned that the Salvation Army had reached its helping hand even to these poor lands. Later, seated in the Salvation Army Hall, amongst a hundred or so of the meanest and poorest kind of people, I faintly realized the real good a few persons of sincere purpose may accomplish, though all odds are against them.

St. Lucia is a typical southern island. Its mountains, clad with great tropical forests and jungles, are the home of many wild animals. Here the English sportsman finds his joy and excitement in hunting the fleet deer, while for still more exciting game, he may hunt the leopard and wild-cat up in the mountains.

Castries, the principal city, off which we were anchored, presented a very pretty sight, the older part being nestled at the base of the mountains, while the

4

newer life seemed to be entwining
itself about the sides of the great precipice.

Towards evening the great cables
which had been holding the *Madiana*
to the pier were loosened and we drifted
once again into the open harbor. We
had been given a farewell by the inhabitants of the town who came down
to the wharf, the negroes, gaudily
dressed, looking like parrots in crim-
sons, blues, and greens.

A little later we were passing the
Pitons, two great volcanic mountains
rising perpendicularly from the water
to a height of about three thousand feet.
The sea about these cliffs is so deep that
a steamer could pass touching the very
sides of the precipice itself.

A story is told of four English sailors,
who, having heard that these mountains were insurmountable, made oath
among themselves that they would try
to accomplish the feat. Their friends

A BELLE OF ST. LUCIA.

from a boat in the distance watched them anxiously through glasses. When half-way up one of them was seen to drop, but the three others went on. A few hundred feet higher a second dropped, and afterwards a third. The last one had almost reached the summit when he also fell. No account of what had befallen them ever reached the ship. They are supposed to have been bitten by the *fer de lance*, the deadliest snake in St. Lucia and perhaps in the world.

XI

BARBADOES, AN ENGLISH COLONY UP TO DATE

ALL was bustle and commotion on board the *Madiana* on the morning of January 12th, for we were soon to arrive at Barbadoes, which was her last stopping-place before she turned her bow again toward the North. Many of the passengers intended returning to New York again by the *Madiana*; others, like myself, decided to part with the boat, and associations which had become so endeared, and strike out for new regions.

It was with much feeling that I bade adieu to our good captain, Mr. Fraser, and to the passengers who had been with us thus far on the cruise.

Barbadoes is very much unlike the other islands we have visited in being not of the volcanic order but of a coral formation, thus presenting a level appearance. It is about the size of the Isle of Wight, and has a population of about 180,000, by far the greater part blacks.

On arriving at Barbadoes I was at once driven to the Marine Hotel, whither I had sent my luggage. The Marine is a fine old hostelry built of rough stone, a few miles from the town facing the sea. Here one can always find the cool breezes of the ocean and the cleanliness of a well-kept inn. In this vicinity are many of the better houses of the capital and principal city of Barbadoes, Bridgetown. Tramways run from the business part of the town to this locality, a distance of about three miles. At the hotel I afterwards met a few Americans as well as some Britons. People seek this island for its

salubrious climate and its pleasant surroundings.

Barbadoes having been occupied by
the British for some two hundred years,
has a distinctively modern English appearance ; there is considerable wealth
there, for the ancestors of many of its
old English families owned plantations
and slaves.

The parade grounds or Savannah of
the military quarters present a lively
scene in the morning and evening, and
thither I strolled about five o'clock in
the evening with a certain charming
passenger of the *Madiana*, who has been
closely associated with many of my
experiences in the islands. That she
should be popular everywhere is indeed
no wonder. She is a typical American
girl: bright, vivacious, experienced, and,
above all, sincere. It is this kind of
girl that has made the American woman appear as the ideal woman in the
hearts not only of Americans, but also

TRAFALGAR SQUARE, BARBADOES.

of the stolid and easy-going Briton, the
gay and vivacious Frenchman, and the
more romantic and sentimental Spaniard.

The soldiers performing their usual
evening dress drill, presented a fine
view on the field. The infantry per-
formed their evolutions, directed by
officers in gay costumes, while farther
off in the distance the cavalry bore
down upon an imaginary enemy, and
the artillery brought up the rear.

At our first dinner on the island,
among other things on the bill of fare
I noticed flying fish, and as these were
considered a great delicacy, I felt that
I certainly must try them. They taste
very much like the sole of England.
The fish itself is of the same genus as
the flying fish we meet in crossing the
northern Atlantic, but of a much smaller
species.

The next day I took a long drive with
the Count about this section. We drove

past the Government prison and the labor-house, not caring to visit either, as I had been through institutions of a similar nature. Suffice it to say, that the Government institutions are here well cared for. The governor, appointed by the Home Government, is an able man and well qualified for those duties of trust and importance placed upon him by the Queen. There is an assembly which makes the laws and which somewhat corresponds to our Senate and House of Representatives. A chief justice presides over the judicial department, and there are other judges on the bench. The police are well trained, being under the supervision of a Chief of Police, an important personage of the island.

In driving we passed many plantations and rich fields of sugar, rice, and other tropical products. After seeing as much of the country as we had leisure for, we returned to Bridgetown and did some shopping. The shops are very much like those in England and on a grand scale. They have a few large department stores where one can find anything from a hat-pin to an anchor.

We visited the famous Ice-house and drank the local popular drink, the swizzle. The Ice-house, so called because the luxury of ice is there obtained, is common to all the West Indian islands and is a sort of hotel with café and restaurant attached. Here the better elements of the people usually meet and lead that indolent existence common to the South. The swizzle, which is the characteristic drink of the Islands, is a sort of cocktail, which after being concocted is made to ferment by the use of a stick with prongs on the end called a swizzle-stick. It is a mild and cooling drink, in which both the ladies and gentlemen of the South indulge.

That evening I was invited out to dinner by some English friends to whom

I had letters. Their estate, situated a little distance from town on an eminence, affords a fine specimen of colonial architecture, refinement, and wealth. High stone walls encircle the grounds ; fountains give an air of life, while in the rear is a park of great trees. The house is built of rough stone : the rooms are commodious and comfortable. A great entrance hall into which open the rooms, is finished in hard wood, and contains many relics of antiquity, such as helmets, swords, fire-arms, etc. All the rooms contain large fireplaces, for even in this climate the evenings are cool and damp.

After dinner our host, a good story-teller and a man who has had many adventures and experiences, related in an interesting way phases of the life of former days in the Indies and on the Spanish Main.

I must not leave Barbadoes without impressing upon my readers the importance and significance of this island and especially of the city—Bridgetown. This is the centre of trade for all the Islands and the port of the Royal Mail line between England and the Islands and the mainland of South America, as well as that of the Hamburg-American steamers, of other European lines, the Quebec Steamship Co., and the boats plying between South America and New York. It is in fact the New York of the Indies. The city itself is composed of substantial shops and warehouses. The streets are well paved and illuminated by electricity. Here one finds all the modern conveniences and comforts of life. The docks always present a busy scene where one may gain an idea of the commercial importance of the place.

A few days later I boarded the Royal Mail Steamship *Solent*, which was to carry us over our route to Venezuela by way of the islands of Grenada, Trinidad, and Curaçoa; three countries promising much of interest.

It is towards five o'clock in the evening when the *Solent* slowly steams out of the harbor of Barbadoes. I wave a little silk flag with the stars and stripes to our fair companion, who has added so much to the pleasure and interest of this trip and has also endeared herself very greatly to our memory. She is to remain here for some time and enjoy with her father the delightful place, and towards spring is to return once again to her friends and home in the North.

XII.

THE *Solent* is one of those sharp, well-fitted steel cruisers which are so often seen flying the British flag in foreign waters. She is scarcely of three thousand tons, and is said to be the ideal model of the Royal Mail Line. The rooms, though not situated on the upper deck as were those of the *Madiana*, yet are large and comfortable and the table is excellent.

In the evening the captain, the doctor, the purser, and the other officers of the boat appear in full dress. Their example is also followed by the passengers on the boat.

But although so superior to the *Ma-*

diana in respect of discipline and service, I still bear the fondest recollections of the pleasures of that good home-like ship which brought us to Barbadoes.

We had a night of smooth sailing. About four o'clock the next afternoon, after coasting the shores of Grenada for some hours, we turned a point of land and entered the almost perfectly land-locked harbor of the principal city—St. George.

On approaching, the first thing we noticed was a fort built of heavy stone, overlooking the town and the harbor. It seems to be an Englishman's joy to tug and climb whenever an opportunity presents itself. I was soon on my way ashore with four young English fellows from London. The first thing we did on landing was to scale the heights from below and try to gain access to the fort. After an hour's hard work we reached the gate and were accosted by a sleepy sentry. We sent our cards to the commandant of the fort, and in a few minutes one of the lieutenants was showing us about the place.

There is nothing remarkable about the fort. It is a crumbling mass of stone, and the few old rusty cannon lying about could probably not be used even in case of an emergency. The garrison consists of a handful of old crippled men, mostly negroes, and when later I saw them on drill I thought I had never known a poorer show of soldiers who wore the British uniform.

Indeed, there was but little life anywhere to be seen on this island. The citizens of the town lay about in a doleful mood, as if they had forgotten all about such a thing as energy. In former years, before the negro gained so much control over affairs, and when many white people lived on the island, things were prosperous ; the cane-fields were well cultivated and brought in handsome incomes, and commerce and trade were active.

The subject is too sad to linger upon. The few white inhabitants are thoroughly disgusted, and seem to have lost all ambition of bringing about other results.

In contrast to all this, as we were leaving the shores of Grenada, a sunset such as I have never seen in any land before was presented to us. My travelling companion, who had circled the globe twice, told me he had never witnessed its equal. Softly drawn before our eyes as though by some unseen hands, the spectrum of the sun in hues of soft radiance and beauty lingers a few moments before all is dark.

XIII.

TRINIDAD—FIRST GLIMPSES

IT is the early dawn of a tropical morning. For some hours our boat, the *Solent*, has been skirting the shores of the beautiful island of Trinidad. Then, as if in response to the morn's welcome, we proudly steam into the harbor. The peace of the island is slowly awakened by the soft caressing rays of the golden sun ; as though afraid to disturb such tranquillity, its disk lingers behind the three great peaks which suggested to Columbus the Trinity and gave to the island its name— Trinidad.

We were soon being rowed to shore by half a dozen strong negroes. It must be remembered that in these immediate waters, where the dredging machine is still unknown, a ship dares not approach too near the shore.

The streets of Port au Spain, the capital and chief city of the island, are well laid out, and we were surprised at the commercial importance a city in this far out of the way land can attain. Large business houses, the results of modern civilization, are on either side of the street, and we were passing an intelligent-looking people, with an air of refinement, worldliness, and culture, far different from what one generally sees in these southern countries. Thanks be to England, for she has planted in this remote corner of the globe the civilization and advantages of modern Europe.

Yet in sharp contrast to all this, and what appeared to me to be as incongruous as would the slow lengthy treading of a camel on Broadway, are the East

Indian coolies engaged in their daily
routine of work.   Had we not been prepared for such a scene it must have indeed startled us.   The first question a
person asks is, How does the coolie find
himself on these shores?   England, re-
alizing the necessity of agricultural de-
velopment, and finding a scarcity of
good labor in Trinidad, took advantage
of the unique opportunity which presented itself in the transplanting of these
people from the far East to another
Southern home.

The contract which the planter who
imports these coolies through the Government must enter into, is made first
with the Government itself, and secondly
with the coolie.   England in the case
of the coolie maintains herself rightful
protector against his master, in much
the same way as she extends protector-
ate over foreign colonies in Africa,
though on better grounds.   The coolie
must be well cared for by the master, to

whom he is indentured for a term of
five years, after which he is free to
choose his own course. During the
time of his indenture he is paid about
thirteen cents for each working day,
six days in the week being stipulated
as the number the coolie must work.
After the expiration of his time he may
be transported back to India, if he so
choose, or, what is more frequently the
case, for a small sum he may buy considerable ground from the Government
and enter into the farming business for
himself.   In the allotment of the coolies
after their importation from India, great
care is taken not to break up families.
On the whole, this arrangement seems
a commendable one, doing well for
the coolie, who is overburdened and
poverty-stricken in his over-populated
home, and bringing him to a country of
vast resources and great wealth, which
is only waiting to be developed. There
are many thousands of coolies living in

Trinidad, besides a great many in British Guiana and other South American countries.

We paid a visit to the Trinidad Club, finding that club life in the West Indies is an important factor in the better class of society. Here one will sometimes encounter people such as one finds at the Savoy in London, and the Opera in Paris, and meets in the best drawing-rooms both in Europe and America. The clubs are very much the same as those we are accustomed to, with this great advantage over ours, in being more hospitable and frank, and in general truer to the tastes and desires of gentlemen.

We refreshed ourselves with a light breakfast, taken beneath the dark blue sky on the open verandah. A pleasant and most charming custom indeed! Here, hid by the screenage of rich palms and exotics, lingering over our cigars and coffee, the first officer of the *Solent*

and I decided to spend the day in an
outing among the mountains of this,
the most beautiful island of the Indian
seas.

XIV.

TRINIDAD—WANDERINGS ABOUT PORT AU SPAIN

ONE should not leave Trinidad without spending some time in the places of which Charles Kingsley in his book on the Indies speaks so enchantingly, so our good friend the officer told our negro groom to proceed to these points.

After leaving the club we drove toward the Trinidad market-place, passing through the principal business streets. The tinkling of a bell on a single mule pulling a worn-out looking yellow street-car, reminded us that we were in the land of time and leisure.

I have usually found that the shop

windows in a place show the tastes of its
people, and here, noting the many imported wares on display, it was not hard
to realize that these people, though living in the torrid zone, enjoy the comforts and luxuries of Europe.

After a while we saw a long wooden
building with a great glass roof, and
surrounded by a large yard. This is
the famous market-place. It was still
early in the morning, and hither we
found the coolies coming from the
country, many having walked many
miles to offer their vegetables and wares
for sale. Here were coolies sitting in
the same posture as we find the merchant in Constantinople, and bargaining
in the most decided manner even over
the most trivial things.

They deal in cloth, jewelry, shoes,
hardware, in truth, one could purchase
from them almost anything from an Indian filigree ring to an English sewing
machine. The mass of the people at

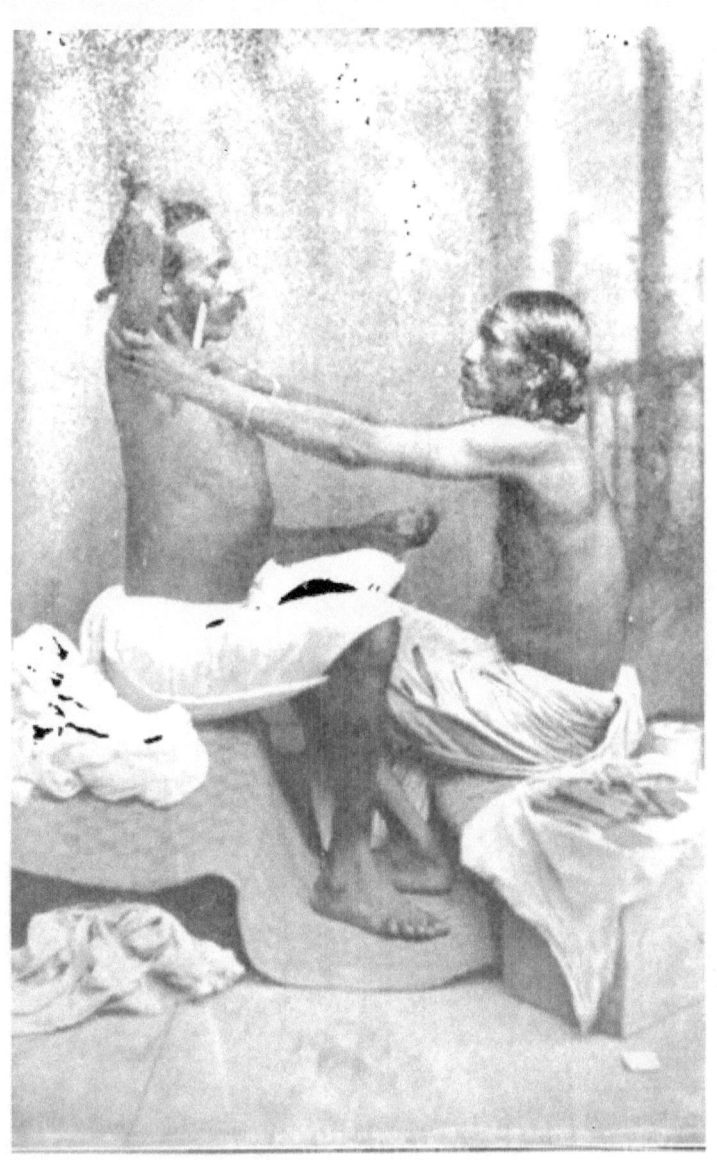

COOLIE BARBERS, TRINIDAD.

the market are coolies, though we noticed a sprinkling of negroes among them.

After purchasing a few odd articles we went on to the museum. Here are all sorts of specimens from the animal, vegetable, and mineral kingdoms, representing both the present and past of the islands. It is thrilling indeed, to hold in one's hand an awful scorpion, the very one perhaps whose bite has sent many to the grave ; or to stroke the boa constrictor, the terror of the people. Many are the stories I heard told during my sojourn in South America of how this reptile, after fascinating its prey, hurls itself upon it, only to result in the sure death of its victim.

Here too were butterflies more beautiful than I had ever imagined, and fossils and shells representing the prehistoric age of the island ; also there lay scattered about the rooms tools and implements belonging to the Stone Age, and showing the customs and arts of the Caribs during that period.

From the museum we drove to the residence part of Port au Spain, skirting the great Savannah on the way. This open space covers a considerable area bordering on the fashionable street leading to the Government House and the Botanical Gardens. It is a place of much importance to the general populace of the city. Here are held the open-air political meetings, the championship tourneys, tennis games, and horse-racing.

The best houses are on the Savannah; it is where the old English aristocracy established itself.

But the old colonial institutions are fast decaying, and the English population now prefer England to Trinidad.

The Government House is the residence of the governor of the island, and is a palace fit for the ruler of any empire. It stands in the midst of a

fine park with fountains, and grounds
for tennis and cricket. Charles Kingsley has made it the background for
many interesting incidents. I was so
fortunate as to attend a ball given by
the governor, in which, under the banner of England, were gathered men and
women from every clime. I met representatives from South America, travel-
lers from the Far East, officers from the
continent of Europe, and other officers
well able to represent the dignity of our
own beloved country. What a scene
for a romance under the palms in the
park that beautiful moonlight night, as
the faint strains of sweet music fell on
the ear! Well, perhaps there was one!

After leaving the Government House
we took a stroll through the Botanical
Gardens. So much has been written
and said of these that I dare say they
are not unfamiliar to my readers. The
Gardens are maintained by the English
Government at a considerable expense.

The chief purpose is to try experiments in the cultivation of different trees, plants, shrubs, and numbers of other sub-divisions of the vegetable kingdom. It is a most important branch of the Department of Agriculture in London. Trinidad has the honor to boast of the grandest and most luxuriant Gardens in the world; although, as mentioned once before in this book, those of Martinique are by their natural advantages very much superior.

It was growing toward noon; the ball of fire above us was asserting itself more and more strongly. The birds in the trees stopped chirruping and betook themselves to rest. Here, in a grove of mangoes overlooking the coffee fields, we made a halt for luncheon.

Luncheon over, our cigars were lighted. The officer began telling me of his travels in the Indian Archipelago; how, when lieutenant of Her Majesty's good ship *Lark*, he was ordered by the captain to make a survey of one of the remote islands. Toward night the party became lost in the thick fogs and underbrush. But I cannot finish the story. I fell asleep at that point and dreamed not of jealous nations ruling the earth and fighting for the balance of power, but of one great land where all is peace and contentment.

XV.

TRINIDAD, A MINIATURE OF HINDUSTAN

I AM awakened from my slumber by my companion, who assures me that it is time for us to start. It is much later and the heat has abated. The soft trade-winds are refreshing. So off we drive through forests of mango and mahogany, skirted by citron and bamboo, to Coolie-Town, and thence to Blue Basin, our final stopping-place. We are no 'longer on the level prairie, but climb the rough roads among the mountains. The slopes, covered with thick tropical vegetation, are luxuriant. We make our way through jungles so thick that it becomes quite dark, and again burst out into the broad daylight. We pass plantations of sugar and coffee. The officer tells me much about these people.

There is almost always a sad expression on their faces. I noticed this even amongst the younger ones; something dreamy and far-away that I could never understand. Could this have been handed down from former generations? The coolies' lot in India has always been a hard one, obliged as they were to suffer from want of food and from the tyrannical rule of a despotic government. Perhaps their patient forbearance has recorded itself in the facial lines of this sad, transplanted people.

The East Indian is a graceful being, soft-skinned, and with movements of perfect ease. The women have long black silky hair which ordinarily they let fall down their backs. Their robe is one of the utmost simplicity and beauty, somewhat resembling the toga of ancient Rome. It is made up of long rolls of white cotton cloth, disposed in graceful folds. The arm is left bare, as well as the upper bosom and the lower half of the limbs. I have seen many of these people wear this simple costume far more gracefully than their northern sisters carry their Worth gowns.

Bracelets, curiously wrought of silver, ornament the arms and lower limbs. One woman I saw wore as many as three dozen. Odd-shaped rings in the likeness of serpents and animals bedeck the fingers and toes. The costume of the men is simple ; trousers of white duck and a short coat, or, more often, mere strips of white cotton about the loins. The latter alone constitutes the costume of a majority of the men.

We have now entered Coolie-Town, so let us dismount and walk about so as to observe the place more closely. This is a miniature of life in India.

The houses are built of bamboo with
open spaces for doors and windows.
Usually the house is divided into two
rooms, one for sleeping and the other
for cooking.   The shops appear the
same as the residence houses.   In front,
by the door, usually sit the merchants.
Among them are many silversmiths engaged in turning silver into rings, bracelets, and other ornaments.   In this we
discover the true cause of the women's
display of jewelry ; it represents the
assets of their husbands' business.

Before leaving the town I observed a
tall man with white robes and graceful,
dignified bearing, enter a large house
built more artistically than the others
and a little apart on a knoll.   Heavy
portières of rich red silk hung about
the large doors.   Something about the
man impressed me very much.   His
face was one of intelligence, learning,
and refinement—the very seat of seri-
ousness.   I paused in front of the place

6

and would probably have entered had not my friend come to me hurriedly and explained that I was standing before the holy temple, and that for one not of their faith to enter is great sacrilege. But through the curtains, left partially open, I saw before the altar men and women in prayer. A faint light is reflected from an old colored bronze lamp, and their gods rest on the table, flowers,—representing life,—being strewed about the room.

Is it not remarkable that these people, after leaving home, friends, and country, should still keep to their religion as closely as ever? The coolie is well built, agile, and graceful. The negro, though powerful, is clumsy and ignorant. No wonder these races do not amalgamate. We hear of no intermarriages, there are no social relations between the two.

In speaking of the coolie, I must not fail to mention his cousins of the far

HINDU RELIGIOUS CEREMONY, TRINIDAD.

East, the Chinese coolies. These too have found a home in Trinidad. Although not so numerous as the East Indians, they are increasing steadily. They take to agriculture, and in disposition are quiet, sullen, or sad. Seldom do we find a smile lighting their countenances.

Taking to our carriage again, we were soon driving through rich tropical forests on our way to Blue Basin. We had not time to visit the famous pitch lake, situated in another part of the island, from which the asphalt used all over the world is mined. The lake is composed entirely of this pitch, and as soon as any is taken away, fresh pitch from underneath arises to take its place.

We pass, on the roadside, fair coolie women, often carrying baskets on their heads. It is a pretty sight to see the look of interest enlivening their faces as we approach, and their gracious nods and smiles.

Thus we travelled on, working our way into the mountains for some time, till, at first faintly, then more clearly, we heard the rush of a great fall of water. Dismounting, we climbed up the mountain side ; there, leaning from a precipice, we saw dashing over a ledge of rocks a stream of silver water which finds peace and quiet in yonder blue pool in the depths below.

But it was getting late and we knew we must not delay. The thick forests of the Indies are not the safest place in the world at night. The soft light of the evening was falling. By the rays of the moon we threaded our way along the road through the forest and up and down the mountains.

Such a scene inspires the sense of awe. As one of our great philosophers said : "Man can best appreciate his insignificance in comparison with the grandeur of Nature."

XVI.

CURAÇAO, THE HOLLAND OF THE SOUTHERN SEAS.

WAFTED by the gentle breeze of the trade-winds a germ of Holland has sprung up in this remote corner of the world ; and like a fresh twig in spring Curaçao has taken' root and flourished in these southern waters. No city I have ever seen so resembles the cities of Holland as Willemstad, the capital. Leading from a lagoon which forms the harbor, canals extend through the city in all directions, with quaint bridges connecting the land on either side. The typical Holland scull-boat has its home in these waters. We see flying in the harbor the flags of all nations. Large iron-clad vessels lie side by side with small sailing craft. Curaçao is the one place among these Islands, outside of St. Lucia, where our boat was able to draw up to the pier.

The houses, too, are an exact reproduction of those built in Holland, with slanting red-tiled roofs, clean white-washed sides, dark green shutters ; and the people themselves dress the same as their brothers across the water. The girls and boys wear the heavy wooden shoes ; the girls look very pretty indeed with that peculiar white linen head-gear of the Dutch, and with their short skirts and white stockings. Many of the men still wear knickerbockers, with silver buttons and white hose.

Curaçao is by far the cleanest and most inviting country I visited on this trip. The very air seems fresh and stimulating in comparison with that experienced elsewhere in these parts.

It was with pleasure I accepted the

A TROPICAL ISLAND SCENE.

invitation of Consul Smith to take a little trip with him in his yacht about the canals and around the shores of the island. We visited cane fields, and orange groves, where the peel of the orange is converted into that famous liqueur called Curaçao.

The island, which is small and for the most part barren, is composed largely of phosphates. These are shipped in large quantities to the different markets of the world, the Government deriving at least half a million dollars a year therefrom.

There is not a spring nor a well there, nor any fresh water, the inhabitants being entirely dependent upon rain-water for existence ; and as it sometimes does not rain for a year or two, the natural supply is often exhausted, and the people are obliged to resort to water brought in barrels by schooners from the Venezuelan coast, fully 90 miles away.

The streets are well-paved and as

clean as the boulevards of Paris. The country roads are hard and well-built. The entire place has about it an air of success. Everybody seems happy and well pleased with life ; how different in this respect from their neighbors the negroes of the Islands ! The greater part of the population of Curaçao is also negro ; but, due partially perhaps to its natural advantages, they seemed to me to be of a more thrifty sort.

At the shops I purchased several bits of jewelry wrought in the peculiar Dutch style. A great many of the names above the shops have a "Van" as a prefix.

There are many churches in Curaçao, and morality is said to have attained a higher degree here than at the other Islands we have visited. As regards the general morality of the West Indies, perhaps it will not be out of place for me to say that the negro's sense of what is right and what is wrong is dictated by his feelings and not by his conscience. His conscience is still in the embryonic condition, and it will require some years of experience to make it strong enough for his actions to be ruled by his mind. A friend of mine who had lived for many years in the Indies and had seen and studied the negro, told me that he would almost as soon leave his family near the dens of wild animals as to leave them on his estate, remote from the foreign settlements, without the presence of himself or his friends. Of course this is exaggerated, but it only tends to show the feelings of the colonist toward the negro.

XVII.

LA GUAYRA—FIRST SCENES IN VENEZUELA

A PUFF of smoke, then a roar which is echoed and re-echoed through the valleys, announced our arrival in Venezuela. Before us rose boldly the mountains of the Northeastern Andes, a Venezuela coast range, crowned by the Silla de Carácas, a peak rising to the height of 8600 feet. The city of La Guayra, which is one of the three principal seaports of Venezuela, lies nestled at the foot of this great ridge of mountains. From our boat in the harbor it looked like a Lilliputian village in the land of the Giants.

There was much official ceremony

and display of military authority connected with our landing, a part of the routine which every one is obliged to go through before he may land in Venezuela.

First a little boat carrying a yellow flag brings on board the quarantine officer. He ascertains from which ports we come, whether all these ports are free from being quarantined, and if there is any sickness aboard. If, after his scrutiny, all is well, we are met by the military officer and then again by the master of the port.

On landing, all our goods must be examined by the custom-house officers. Then each one of us in person must go through an examination, and papers have to be signed. I was saved all these annoyances by my friend the Marquis Montelo, who is a Spaniard by birth and knows well how to handle such people.

The Marquis and I had already decided on the kind of trip we wished to take through Venezuela ; we had arranged, among other things, a visit to the then U. S. Consul, General Thomas, who has been since made minister, so as to ascertain if the presence of yellow fever would keep us away from any of the places we might wish to visit.

On entering the harbor I noticed a huge structure of masonry built for the purpose of breaking the sea as it rolls in towards Macuto,—since Nature has not been kind enough to this seaport town to build it a harbor in which ships can anchor without danger of being injured or going ashore.

This great breakwater was built by an English company, which for its expense and trouble is allowed a certain per cent. of the revenue collected as its share.   I met the manager of the Company, who talked interestingly to me and gave me much information regarding the English, German, and other foreign enterprises in Venezuela. He told me that he regretted having ever sunk any money in Venezuela himself, and that the breakwater was not financially successful. He spoke also of the railroad which runs from La Guayra to Carácas, a distance in a straight line over the mountains of only six miles, but from the necessity of winding around the valley so as to gain access above, the distance is lengthened fourfold. This railroad, likewise, was built by an English syndicate, and, as I later learned in Carácas from Sir Vincent who represented the Company, they were assured a certain per cent. of interest on the money invested, which up to that time, he told me, they had not been able to obtain in full from the Government. It may not be out of place for me to remark here that one of the greatest disadvantages the present Government has to contend with is the existence of contracts and agreements entered into by the previous ruler, President Blanco, with various corporations and syndicates, which are thoroughly impracticable.

After our baggage had been examined it was shipped at once to Macuto, a small town about six miles from La Guayra. Macuto is the Newport of Venezuela, and hither come all the rich and fashionable from Carácas and other cities of the country. As this happened to be the seasonable time, and as the Marquis is well acquainted among the prominent South American families, I agreed with him that it was best to stay at Macuto for a few days before going to Carácas.

On walking up from the quays at La Guayra, I was at once impressed by the typical South American streets, narrow and roughly laid with cobblestones. The houses on both sides seldom stood over two stories, and in many cases the people could shake hands from window to window across the way. There is no regular plan laid out for the streets, but they run in all directions. The city being built at the very base of the great mountains is hilly, in many places even precipitous.

The houses are not well built, being usually of rough stone plastered over with a sort of cement. They are roofed with dirty-looking red tiles, and lack the neat shutters we observed in Curaçao. An iron balcony stands out from the upper windows. This is typical of the South American houses. The shops are not much to boast of. Their articles are displayed in a miscellaneous manner in the windows and lack neatness and system—a characteristic of many of the people also.

La Guayra, being a seaport town, is quite a lively place, and considerable commerce is carried on in coffee, sugar, cocoa, hides, and other products. There are some very large warehouses stocked well with the country's products from all sections.

Public buildings may be seen here and there, but as a whole the city does not present a very picturesque appearance.

We called on our American friend, Mr. Thomas, the United States Consul, and accepted an invitation from him for dinner. His home is situated on the outskirts of the town, on a high hill overlooking the port. It is built in the Spanish style with pretty *patio* or court, having a splashing fountain surrounded by palms and exotics. It is a delightfully cool and remarkably pleasant place.

Before going to Macuto we went to the harbor and bade farewell to our pleasant companions on the *Solent*. The boat grew smaller in the distance until nothing remained but a pleasant memory and a trail of smoke.

XVIII.

MACUTO, THE NEWPORT OF VENEZUELA

THE small dark cars which carried us to Macuto corresponded with the railroad itself, which had been built some years ago, and was a tumble-down, shaky affair.

Macuto lies only about six miles from La Guayra, yet it took us nearly an hour to reach our destination. The engine broke four times on the way thither, and each time all the passengers took a hand in repairing. To call the two rails that run side by side parallel would be offering insult to geometry.

This was my first experience on a South American railway, but later the

railroads which run into the country
for long distances and over dangerous
passes astonished me. The great feats
of civil engineering and the expendi-
ture in making these roads are something for Venezuela to boast of.

Arriving at Macuto, we took quarters
at a hotel facing the sea, the principal
feature of the same being a wide veranda
running all the way around, giving it
the appearance of an Italian villa.
Although rather roughly built, yet the
delicate colors in which it is painted
and the artistic manner in which the
rooms open upon the verandas, together
with its situation at the base of the
great mountains, make it a charming
place indeed.

At dinner I noted a man of very
striking appearance, a tall and handsome young fellow of thirty. His face
showed that he had endured considerable hardships, and his chin had that
strength which suggested the idea of

his having come out successfully to his own liking. I noticed that he wore a college pin. This brought back to me my own school days and at once put us on terms of friendship. He had returned a few days before from the gold fields of the Orinoco, where he had spent much of his time for the last ten years. His health failing him at college, and his father's business at the same time doing likewise, he was compelled to fall back on his own resources. Leaving the luxuries of the life he had been accustomed to, he worked his way in canoes with two Englishmen and some Indians up the Orinoco on their way to the gold fields. The first year was unsuccessful, and except for reinforcements the idea would have been abandoned ; but gold having been found all through that section of the country, they still worked diligently in the search. Twice was he taken down with fever, and the entire party was in-

jured by sickness ; the country, morever,
was infested with reptiles and wild animals, and many of the roving Indians
in that territory were unfriendly to
strangers. Such is a brief outline of
the story he told me. He was now
quite satisfied with what he had accomplished, and, as vice-president of one
of the large mining companies, was
returning to New York. I learned
from him much that was of interest in
connection with the disputed territory
of this section, the accuracy of which
was afterwards confirmed by the American Minister.

There are many parks in Macuto,
whose natural beauty is enhanced by
art, in which the young people take
great pleasure. After the surf-bathing,
which takes place at about ten o'clock
in the morning, the ladies all array
themselves in light gowns with large
sun-bonnets and listen to the military
band playing in the Plaza. Hither

also stroll the beaux of the place, and there is an informal greeting and general good time. About an hour later the ladies disappear, and are not again seen in public until, say, five o'clock, when the band again plays in the Plaza and the fair maids, arrayed this time entirely in black, their heads adorned with the Spanish mantilla, present a more formal aspect.

Spanish is the language spoken, and although I believed myself to have acquired some knowledge of it while in Mexico and other Spanish-speaking countries, I was frequently at fault to express my thoughts. Some of the girls I met were able to speak a little French or German. One of these, in whose company I found myself frequently, who had had the advantages of a Paris education, helped me considerably. There was one phrase in my Spanish-American guide-book which I always repeated shortly after an introduction, with my best accent. The phrase read " *Vd* (*usted*) *es muy amable*," meaning "You are charming," rightly opining that these Southern queens are just as susceptible to kind phrases as are their Northern sisters.

It was with the most pleasant recollections and kindest feelings that we bade adieu to our friends in Macuto, a few days later, when we left for Caracas, a gem in the Andes.

XIX.

CARACAS, A CAPITAL IN THE VENEZUELAN ANDES.

WITH the tooting and screeching of our English locomotives and the ringing of gongs we departed Monday afternoon from the railroad station at La Guayra for Caracas.

The cars were typical English coaches and the locomotives also were English built. Telegraph and telephone lines also are in operation in all the principal cities of Venezuela. A few minutes' ride brought us to the crest of the hill overlooking the city, from whence we obtained a bird's-eye view of the place at which we had spent the last few days. But it was not until some minutes afterward, in winding our way up the steep precipices, thousands of feet above the sea, that we appreciated the magnitude of this railroad enterprise and its marvels of engineering and construction. The St. Gothard Pass in Switzerland is nothing in comparison, neither is Georgetown in Colorado, nor the Mexican Railroad which thunders down the mountains from the City of Mexico on its way to Vera Cruz. Like flies on a wall we scaled the dizzy precipice. The mountains extended as far as the eye can reach in either direction, while back of us, thousands of feet below, rolled the blue sea with here and there a white speck signifying a ship bound for a distant port.

When a little later our train climbed over the crest, there lay before us the beautiful valley of the Rio Guaire with the fair city of Caracas in its midst.

We were soon lodged in our comfortable quarters at the Grand Hotel, where

I met an old travelling companion. We three had a pleasant dinner, comparing notes of travel and discussing the recent topics of the day, both in Europe and America.

The Marquis called me betimes the following morning, as we had many places to visit and much to do the next few days before leaving Caracas. We took a Venezuelan breakfast, which consists only of chocolate or coffee, rolls, and cheese. This is called the early breakfast. Toward noon the substantial breakfast is served, which is very much the same as their later dinner. I have noticed as many as eight or sometimes ten courses being served at ordinary hotels at these breakfasts and dinners. As a rule the cooking in Venezuela and the other South American countries is typically Spanish. They seem to know no limit to the use of peppers, garlic, onions and the like, which are apt to spoil a foreigner's stomach if he is not very careful. The chilliness of the King of Tabasco might well be relieved by the seasoning of South American food.

A very pretty custom observed in these countries is to serve the meals in an open patio. At dinner this is especially pleasant, under the blue canopy of heaven set with twinkling stars. Music is usually near to lend its soft charm to the hour.

After the light breakfast we started out on our wanderings. My first impressions of Caracas came in the form of an agreeable surprise. I had always heard of this as one of the most beautiful cities in South America, yet I had not conceived of the grandeur and taste that could be displayed in building a city in this remote corner of the globe. At the intersections of the streets are pretty plazas, the most important being the Plaza Bolivar, which is quite near to the four principal business streets of

CARACAS, VENEZUELA, GENERAL VIEW.

the city.   Richard Harding Davis well
called Caracas   the Paris of South
America.

What a foreigner first notices is the
decidedly French air of the city.   The
very names above the shops and the
signs naming the articles for sale are in
French.   French bonnets, gowns, neck-
wear, etc., adorn the shop windows.
There are also a few German enterprises
in Caracas, but more especially among
the larger wholesale dealers.

American interests are steadily growing in Venezuela.   One of the most
prominent names in commercial and
general importance in Caracas is that
of my pleasant acquaintance, Mr. Henry
Boulton, who, with his brothers, is a
large importer of grain, breadstuffs, and
other commodities, and in return exports
great quantities of coffee, cocoa, hides,
and other Venezuelan products.   These
brothers now run a splendidly equipped
line of steamers between Venezuela and

New York, and it is due to their energy and perseverance that a large share of the trade relations between the United States and Venezuela have been brought about. The Boultons have been conducting business between these two countries for many years, dating back to the thirties, when only small sailing sloops were engaged for the purpose.

The city of Caracas I found clean and well kept, from the public buildings to the streets themselves. The fresh invigorating air, sweeping down from the Coast Range breathes a life of restlessness and independence into these people. It is no wonder that they were among the first to throw off the yoke of tyranny and subjection.

The residence houses of Caracas are principally one story high, built of adobe walls sometimes two or three feet thick, having windows with iron gratings and broad sills where it is the custom late in the afternoon for the pretty señoritas to sit, arrayed in becoming toilets, observing the passers-by and chatting with their friends.

The interior of the houses is always in sharp contrast with their exterior. The latter is modest and of rough appearance, but entering the short hallway into the patio, is like going into a different world. The patio, which usually has a fountain, is surrounded by palms, ferns, and other tropical plants. Broad stone hallways lead from its space to the different rooms through arches graceful with ivy and other creeping vines. I have been in some houses in Caracas the interiors of which were decorated in the most artistic and luxurious manner, Turkish rugs covering the floors and tapestries bedecking the walls. The water supply of the city is brought from the mountains by means of aqueducts, constructed by the former president, Guzman Blanco. Tramways traverse some of the streets. Many shops bear an air of foreign relationship, and the cafés have adopted the French custom of setting small tables on the broad sidewalks, where it is usual for persons to sit and read during the long days, sipping the different beverages of the country.

On the outskirts of the town there is a sort of park called El Puente Hierro, which has been much improved of late years. Here are many cafés, dance-halls and other delights for frivolous pleasure-seekers. On Sunday afternoon it is the fashion to take a drive to this park, when the ladies of the better class sit in their carriages and listen to the music, while the peons, swelling the crowd and paying their few coppers here and there, have a great holiday.

The people of Venezuela do not seem to know what we would call a good horse. A gentleman at whose home I visited, showed me a horse which he had imported from Peru which was consid-

ered a grand specimen. He had paid
two thousand dollars for the animal,
but I much doubt if the same one would
have brought more than two hundred at
the New York Horse Exchange.

Many of the private carriages are
made in France, usually built in the
style of our victorias, and are certainly
good looking. The horses are small,
resembling our Western ponies. The
bicycle was then almost unknown here,
as in many other places in South America, although I saw one or two, which
were such curiosities that people stopped
their work to follow the machines, and
the urchins of the streets ran after them
shouting and yelling.

The president lives in an unpreten-
tious house not far from the business
part of the city. In sharp contrast to
the modest appearance of his home, and
the genuineness and unpretentiousness
of the man, is the ostentatious military
display with which he is surrounded. A

group of trusty cowboys, mounted on horses and armed with carbines and revolvers, form his especial body-guard and follow him everywhere. The president told me that some of these men had been through many daring engagements with him, and would willingly, at any moment, sacrifice themselves for the life of their ruler. He is now having built, on a hill overlooking the city, a beautiful house of white stone. President Crespo is a man of very moderate tastes and is probably spending so much money on his home less for his own gratification than in order to have his surroundings more in accordance with his position. He has won the favor of the people by living an unassuming life, thus coming into closer connection with the masses.

PRESIDENT CRESPO, OF VENEZUELA.

XX.

CARACAS—REFLECTIONS ON THE PAST AND PRESENT.

THE day had been unusually close, the sun shining through a cloudless sky. Toward evening, the earth groaned forth its sighs of agony. The people rushed from their homes and places of amusement only to be dashed to the ground and crushed beneath the ruins of their crumbling city. Such was the sight on the 26th of March, 1812, when the great earthquake surprised the city and destroyed twelve thousand of its people.

Vainly did the Spanish rulers of the province use their cunning and deceit in trying to make the superstitious people of Venezuela believe this an act of God to show his vengeance on their uprising against their mother-country.

It was but a year previous, on the 5th of July, that the great Miranda, then of middle age, stood before a document which he had drawn up, and with other patriotic men of his country signed a declaration of independence for the people of Venezuela. This was the first formal proclamation of independence, which was soon after to bring many into battle and cause a great loss of life and property.

Much might be said about Miranda, whose life from beginning to end was like an invention of romance. It was he, who, coming over with Lafayette, helped fight for the American colonies against the British crown. His name can be no more suitably commented upon than by placing it side by side with that of Bolivar, the great Liberator of South America.

It is needless to speak of Bolivar, who spent his life in the cause of his country, leading on the revolutionists to victory after victory. He starved along with the soldiers, and tramped through jungles in the fierce tropical sun, sharing the common lot of all ; and at last, through his high aims and lofty character, accomplished for South America the liberation and independence of five of its great countries.

The Palacio Federal, which is at present used as the Capitol building of Venezuela, is a large picturesque structure, whose rooms are fitted in an appropriate manner. Here are paintings of the many presidents of Venezuela, and of various generals and soldiers who fought in the cause of their country. One could spend weeks studying the relics of the past in connection with things of the present. I passed a few hours in this building in company with that eminent scholar and scientist, Dr.

Adolph Ernst, the greatest savant of Venezuela, and a man of high reputation in the scientific circles of both Europe and America.

While in Caracas one should not fail to visit the home of Guzman Blanco, situated in the suburb of Antimino. It is a palace fit for a czar or emperor. Surrounded by parks of rare beauty, and in itself a grand and stately home, it presents a unique appearance to the visitor. The presidents have all had their hands quite full in maintaining their hold of office. Continuous warfare, due to partisan jealousies and petty ambitions, waged for the last seventy-five years, has kept the country from progressing more rapidly.

As soon as a president is firmly seated a new man will spring up and claim the power. Such has been the common experience in past years. Guzman Blanco alone ruled for nearly twenty years of comparative quiet and peace.

The population of Caracas now numbers about eighty thousand, while the country of Venezuela numbers some two and a half millions. Of the eighty thousand, six thousand are foreigners. It is said that Venezuela has fewer inhabitants than half a century ago, and we can well see that when the fathers and their sons who are old enough are engaged in bitter war there is no chance for the population to increase.

It was under President José Gregorio Monagas, in March, 1854, that the slaves were liberated, and thus the country did away with one of the great barbarisms of the age. Too much stress cannot be laid upon this important fact.

The color line, while at present still noticed in Venezuela, is not nearly so marked as in the countries of the North. Here are often found inter-marriages, and it is no breach of social propriety for a white person to marry one having a taint of colored blood.

Nearly twenty years after the emancipation of the slaves and shortly after Guzman Blanco was made president, he expelled the monks and nuns from the country. Some two or three years later, that wise and far-seeing president, vexed at certain actions of the Archbishop, and seeing that the Church of Rome was becoming a strong feature and a ruling power of the State, expelled the Archbishop and papal nuncio. Shortly after this he issued that famous circular which caused the world to look at him more than ever. It set forth that religious actions are free to everybody, and that he as president could not allow to any one religion advantage over another.

That there are many churches in Caracas, the continual chiming of bells both day and night is sufficient to attest. The cathedral, a large building of no especial beauty, dates back to the 17th century.

A newspaper in a foreign land is always of interest. There are seven news-papers in the city of Caracas, and a few of the dailies are especially good as re-gards the domestic events of the day, though I must say their foreign news is rather scanty.

Caracas has some pretty suburbs, among which might be named Antimino, where President Blanco had his former home ; also El Calvario, a fine park on a hill overlooking the town.

Before leaving the streets of Caracas I must not fail to mention a custom the people have of naming their shops. On the signs we read such names as " Isle of Emerald," " The Fountain of Glad-ness," and others still more odd. Some-thing similar to this, is the custom of naming the children after patron saints. It is not uncommon to hear a mother call her boy across the street " Blessed Peter," " Jesus," or other names taken from the Bible. It is also customary on the baptism of a child to choose a godfather for it. He is supposed to care for the child, and acts in very many respects the same as the natural parent, and it is quite true that there is almost as much affection shown between god-parent and god-son as between father and son.

One evening the Marquis and myself went to the Theatre Municipal. It has a seating capacity of 2500 and is built with much refinement of taste. As in some foreign theatres, the lower galleries are divided into boxes. In the rear, and directly opposite to the stage, is the president's private box, where I saw the president in company with his wife and suite enjoying the performance. The parquet seems to be occupied only by men, who ordinarily do not come in evening dress, although the people in the boxes are expected to be thus attired.

That the Southern peoples are music-lovers has been often noted. The

smallest city of Mexico and South
America will have a military band,
quite the equal of our best bands.
There seems to be a musical sentiment
inborn in these people which has þeen
developed into genuine appreciation of
the art.

On Thursday evenings the Government military band plays in the Plaza,
where, coquettishly wandering in the
shadows, the señoritas respond to their
suitors. Before North American customs became introduced into Caracas,
love-making among the best classes
of Venezuelans was European in character. The suitor might not call on his
lady unless some member of the family
was present, even down to the very day
of the marriage, and a breach of this
custom was reason enough to lose the
respect of one's friends. But now more
natural manners in this respect have
superseded the old, and the cavalier
sends his card to the lady upon whom

he wishes to call, just as in the United States.

While the band is playing the national anthem, I walk with my friend to another park. This plaza has no pretty-colored tiles, but instead there is a carpet of velvet grass; and instead of fancy posts and lamps, the solemn palm holds sway. On this night, as the breeze carries to us the strains of the patriotic hymn, we stop before a statue of George Washington erected by General Blanco after his visit to the United States some years ago. As we stand in silence we cannot help feeling a strong sympathy and affection for the people of Venezuela, who have fought for independence much in the same way as did our ancestors.

XXI.

RAILROADING IN VENEZUELA

AFTER having spent a week in Caracas, I decided to bid adieu to my friend the Marquis and investigate further regarding the country and its people. There were rumors afloat of yellow fever raging in the districts I intended travelling through, and it was with no little anxiety that the evening before leaving, while calling at the United States Minister's house, I inquired regarding the report. It was a great relief to be informed that the health of the country was normal and that I need feel no special uneasiness.

There are of course nearly always sporadic cases of yellow fever in the tropics. I shall never forget one evening when I entered Vera Cruz from the City of Mexico. I had intended making connection with the French Transatlantic boat on the way to Cuba, but through miscalculations was obliged to remain for some time in this coast town. It was during the epidemic of yellow fever, and the papers reported each day a long list of the new victims. Such experiences are not very frequent, but after one has passed through them safely, it tends toward making him—I would not say more reckless, but less inclined to credit rumors, most of which when tested prove to be untrue.

The railroad between Caracas and Valencia is owned and operated by German capitalists. It makes a day's journey through one of the most interesting countries I have ever visited. Soon after leaving Caracas the road winds about the mountains. The fierce puffing and steaming of the locomotive

RAILROADING IN VENEZUELA.

shows we are climbing a very steep grade. Now the train crosses deep ravines spanned by iron bridges which look in comparison with the heights like filigree-work. Another time it flanks the side of some deep ravine whose slopes are clothed with thick jungles and forests that spread a shade of darkness over all, or, again climbing the summits of highest mountains, over roads which show the marvellous ingenuity of the civil engineer.

After the first few hours thus spent, we entered a somewhat less hilly country. Green valleys and well-cultivated coffee plantations spread before us like a panorama.

Thanks to these and other railroads which are soon to be constructed, the vast resources and riches of the country will be brought into closer touch with those great winged messengers of our civilized world, the ocean steamers.

It is curious to note how slow and ob-

stinate the peons are about adopting the
customs and conveniences of civilization. Yet this trait is in accord with
the nature and habit of the general population of South America. Many of
these Venezuelans prefer to ride for
days on the back of a miserable little
burro, climbing dangerous paths, rather
than submit to modern civilization and
avail themselves of the conveniences of
the railroad. I have noticed many long
trains of *burros,* heavily laden with
coffee, cocoa, and other articles of the
country, slowly and with difficulty bearing their produce to the market, although it might just as well and more
cheaply have been sent over the rail.

Before passing from the mountain regions I must not forget to make mention
of the great South American eagle which
we saw soaring high into the clouds
and then floating leisurely along. It is
among these mountains that the true
sportsman most revels. Before my visit

to Venezuela the fiercest game I had ever hunted was the wildcat, or the bear ; now I can better appreciate the feelings with which an African or South American traveller relates his tales of adventure.

The distance of the stations apart depends upon the country through which the road passes. One often rides many miles without coming to a stop. It must be remembered that a great part of Venezuela is still unexplored, and a greater part is uninhabited. A country with an area of six hundred thousand square miles and a population of only about two and a half million is indeed sparingly peopled. The principal export is coffee, which reaches the value of many million dollars annually. Other exports are cocoa, hides, skins, feathers, rubber, and gold.

On leaving Caracas the cars were rather well filled, but towards afternoon there were comparatively few passengers remaining, most of them having reached their destination at some of the smaller stations. It was late in the afternoon before we skirted the shores of Lake Valencia, one of the largest bodies of water in Venezuela, whose shores have been the scene of several bloody engagements during revolutions. There are a few small villages beside it, a rough boat plying between them, but, in correspondence with the rest of the country, it is little utilized.

A complete system of long-distance telephones operates between cities and towns along the line. One can telephone from Valencia to Caracas, with less difficulty than from New York to Chicago. It is quite surprising to see how quickly the people have taken to the telephone ; a great many of the residences both in Caracas and Valencia have their long-distance wires.

It was growing dusk ; the latter part

of the journey had been rather lone-
some, travelling over the great rolling
country. I knew comparatively little
of the places I was about to visit, and
with the vague rumors of yellow fever
still in my ears, I began to wish that I
were back in Chicago or New York.
At the last station the passengers sitting behind me vacated their seats.
While meditating in this way I did not
at first notice a new passenger. After
a little, the car coming to a stop with
an abrupt jerk, I turned around. I
could not see the man's face, as it was
covered by a newspaper he was reading,
but there appeared in large heavy print
on the side of the sheet facing me the
words : "The Chicago Sunday *Trib-
une*." Having met but few Americans
since my arrival in Venezuela, to be
confronted during this day-dream of
mine by a man who, ten chances to
one, was from the same city as myself,
was indeed a queer coincidence. In

9

true American style, I reached over and presented my card, and soon was in conversation with Mr. Russell, an American from Chicago travelling in Venezuela.

XXII.

DARKNESS has covered the country and only after long intervals there shines out a faint gleam from some miserable hut. The train rushes on through the wilderness for hours, until far off in the distance below us appear the many lights of the city of Valencia.

With the ringing of bells and the noisy rumbling of the cars the train rushes into the station. This is the terminal of the German railroad between Caracas and Valencia.

The keeper of the hotel, a good-natured, stout Spanish woman, gave me the key to my apartments, and it was so large and heavy that, while passing through the dark, cold stone halls, I could not help thinking what a useful weapon of defence it would be in case of necessity. The hotels are seldom more than two stories high, and this one was no exception. A military band was playing a Spanish air in the plaza opposite, while the inevitable señoritas, robed in their attractive gowns, promenaded leisurely about. Bringing a large easy chair out on the veranda outside my apartments, I lighted my pipe and enjoyed the unique surroundings of my first night in Valencia.

Soon afterwards I was asleep on the typical bed of South America. It had a canopy at the top from which fine netting hung down around the four sides. When the sleeper is comfortably situated for the night this is tucked in at the sides of the bed, thus forming a protection from the mosquitoes, gnats, and other insects so disagreeable in the South.

In a book I had recently read on Venezuela the writer said that Valencia is the most beautiful city in South America, or at least in Venezuela. I dissent entirely. I think Caracas by far the grander, owing chiefly to its situation, although Valencia is by no means to be despised. Surrounding the entire city loom up the great crests of the Cordillera Range, while in the farther distance, reflecting the sun, are the higher mountains.

One South American city is very much like another. The market-places are interesting features of all. So are the churches, the pleasant parks, and those oddities which have been mentioned in previous chapters. The better residence section of Valencia is situated in a suburban district about two miles away. Connecting this with the main city are small tramway cars drawn by mules, which a peon causes to gallop along in the hot sun, thus making good speed between the two places. Here there are very many pretty villas surrounded by parks. Even the most ordinary of these presents an attractive appearance.

There are always some soldiers to be seen in Valencia. The uniform of the Venezuelan soldiers consists of bright red trousers and a short blue coat. Usually these warriors present anything but an impressive appearance, for they pay little attention to their attire or the way they carry themselves. The equipment of the president's guard differs to the extent of wearing white duck suits and high black boots, with a short sabre and carbine.

There are direct lines of communication connecting Valencia with the other principal cities of Venezuela. The Bank of Venezuela has a branch in Valencia. The city has many large mercantile houses and warehouses of importance, for in the immediate neighborhood is one of the most fertile sections of Venezuela.

To the westward and farther south the country is still largely unknown. Vast forests and jungles, the home of the leopard and panther, occupy much of the territory.

Valencia is the second city of the Republic in size, and has about forty thousand inhabitants.

After spending a few days in this beautiful city, I left one afternoon on the railroad for Puerto Cabello, the seaport town of this part of Venezuela. From thence the boat sails to the wild district of Maracaibo, from which place connections are made with steamers sailing eastward along the Spanish Main and Trinidad to the Orinoco.

The railroad connecting Valencia with the seaport town of Puerto Cabello is owned and controlled by British capitalists. While the engineering and construction are less daring than those of

the road between La Guayra and Caracas, still the region which it traverses
is one of grandeur.

On the verge of this mountainous
district, where the coffee plant covers
the slopes and the cocoa is cultivated
in the valleys to perfection, is the interesting village of San Esteban. It has
been founded principally by the German population of Puerto Cabello, and
here, within a short distance from the
city, the wealthy people of Puerto
Cabello have their homes, preferring the
delightfully cool climate found here to
the hot and unhealthy coast regions.

It was towards nine o'clock when the
train reached Puerto Cabello. The
most notable part of the journey is the
gradual rise of the thermometer until,
on reaching the city itself, the heat is
almost suffocating. Situated as it is in
an indentation of the coast, where the
winds cannot reach it, the heat is something terrific.

Puerto Cabello, the Spanish for the queer title, The Port of a Hair, is so called on the pretence that within its safe harbors a ship might almost be tied by so frail a tether as a hair. This is one of the few places on the coast where a boat can draw up alongside the pier. It is a busy place, about fifteen million pounds of coffee, to mention one thing, being shipped annually. It is the second port in commercial importance in Venezuela. Of its inhabitants, about seven thousand in number are mainly engaged in the commerce of the exporters and importers. Eight different steamship lines ply regularly between this port and England, France, Germany, Holland, the United States, and the West Indes. There are many Germans, as well as other foreigners, among the residents. Puerto Cabello has been made interesting by the many thrilling incidents before and during the Revolution. It was in this hot territory that Sir Francis

Drake, the great English buccaneer, after exploring the coast, succumbed to yellow fever.

At the entrance to the harbor, nearly opposite the city, is the old fort where Simon Bolivar, the Liberator of Venezuela, was placed in command when twenty-six years of age by General Miranda, who was then leading the country in its first struggle for liberty. In the dark dungeons of the fort were gathered the Spanish prisoners and officials seized by the revolutionary party. Bolivar had a sub-lieutenant in whom he placed great confidence. It was the treachery of this man that caused Bolivar his first misfortune. The lieutenant was bought over by the other party, and one night let the prisoners free. Young Bolivar escaped in the nick of time, and after swimming several miles to shore, found refuge in a hut farther down the coast, while all the ammunition and arms captured by the insurgents again fell into the hands of the Spaniards. Part of the fort is now used as a prison and hospital, and another portion of it as a barrack, where a handful of soldiers are stationed. It is situated on a low island, on the borders of which grow palms and underbrush. To this place I saw consigned every evening gangs of criminals whose feet were chained and weighted by great iron balls to prevent them from escaping during the time they were at work sweeping the streets, building, dredging, or such other labors as might be assigned to them.

With the quaint City of Puerto Cabello to our left, and the fort to our right, one evening the cables are silently lifted from the pier and our boat glides out to the open sea.

XXIII.

FROM Puerto Cabello the Red " D " line sends a small steamer westward, skirting the shores of the Gulf of Venezuela for some miles until the strait of Maracaibo is reached, entering which, and turning southward, the boat finds its way into the lake of Maracaibo.

This lake is a magnificent body of fresh water with an area of two thousand square miles. The basin is almost anywhere navigable for small vessels. The town of Maracaibo, situated on the western side of the strait which forms the entrance to the lake, is the emporium of the whole region of the eastern Cordilleras, including districts in Colombia.

At the close of the 15th century, when the spirit of adventure and romance filled the heart of every grandee of Spain and every Italian navigator—in those grand old days, Americus Vespucci sailed across the sea in search of new lands. After coasting the shore he entered this beautiful strait and found there, built on piles and rafts, a strange city, where the natives were paddling about in canoes. It reminded the explorer so much of the city of Venice, in his native Italy, that he called it Little Venice, since altered to Venezuela. Even now, situated a little distance from Maracaibo, the city Vespucci described, is another city called Santa Rosa, where the natives still build their houses on rafts, like those of the lake regions around the City of Mexico.

There is nothing of special interest about Maracaibo. It is a city of thirty thousand inhabitants, and of consider-able commercial importance. The riv-ers of the United States of Colombia flow into the lake, and these rivers and good mule-roads make it a centre of commerce. Among the notable build-ings are the palace of the governor, the federal college, custom-house, market-place, theatre, and churches. The city has about ten miles of street railway, and in sharp contrast with its romantic surroundings are abundant telephones and electric lights.

Some distance inward, back of Mara-caibo, is a town called Santa Marta, behind which rises the Nevada peak, said to be the highest on the coast. This is the most easterly port of Colom-bia, and is noteworthy from the fact that Bolivar took refuge and died here when driven into exile by Paez.

Leaving Maracaibo, the boat sails eastward for several days along the Spanish Main. Passing between the

island of Curaçao and Venezuela, and
again. sailing by the towns of Puerto
Cabello and La Guayra, the steamer entered the beautiful straits separating the
island of Margarita from the peninsula
of Paria. This island has been made
famous to the world for the numerous
beautiful pearls found along its coast.
Here the Indians in olden times, with
their crude diving apparatus, risked
their lives in waters infested by sharks
and other man-eating fish, to carry on
trade with the foreigners for articles
which they valued more than pearls.

Some hours after sailing by this beautiful mountainous island of Margarita
the boat entered the capital of Trinidad, Port au Spain, which we had visited on our downward cruise. From
here a small side-wheel American boat,
such as are used on the Mississippi
and other Western rivers, left Port au
Spain, and steamed through the bay
into the mouth of the Orinoco, several

days later reaching Ciudad Bolivar. The boats are owned by North Americans and are manned by American crews.

It is only in the latter part of the journey to Ciudad Bolivar that one begins to realize the beauty of this romantic river, and not until many miles farther up does it attain its highest grandeur. On entering the mouth the banks are low and marshy. Great forests extend back on either side for many miles. Once in a while one sees villages built upon piles in the marshes, the sides of the houses composed of thatched leaves, and roofed with bark, where those simple people live who lead a wild adventurous life in canoes on the waters.

The time required to make the journey to Ciudad Bolivar depends upon the season of the year. Between May and October, when there is a rise in the river of many feet, navigation is much easier than at low water, and the time required

CARIB INDIANS, ORINOCO DISTRICT, VENEZUELA.

is three days.   During the dry season much more time is necessary.

Ciudad Bolivar is situated 240 miles from the sea, where the river is four and a half miles wide and navigable for steamers.   It is very like to the other Venezuelan cities. The volume of business is enormous compared with the population of the country.

In the last few years the export of gold has been valued high in the millions. Cigar manufacturing is carried on to a large extent.   Great warehouses containing stores from the interior give evidence of its commercial importance.

Ciudad Bolivar is the only city properly speaking in a district covering half the territory of Venezuela. The residents are Spanish, German, Italian, and negroes from the Indies. All there is of interest here can be seen in a few days.

Flowing into the Orinoco at various distances are many streams, some deep

10

and extending far into the mountains.
One, the Meta, flows within two days' distance of Bogota, the capital of Colom-
bia, and is so far navigable for small
boats.   Another, the Cassiquiare, flows
towards the Amazon, and by a sort of
natural canal, actually connects the
Amazon with the Orinoco, so that a
small boat entering the Gulf of Paria,
which is the mouth of the Orinoco,
can work its way up the Orinoco and
come out through the mouth of the
Amazon.

Baron von Humboldt in 1808 made a
journey along the entire course of the
Orinoco.   In 1848 Dr. Schomburgk
made a careful journey of investiga-
tion, and wrote a very extended and
valuable book on the country.   This
book with its maps has come into question frequently during the recent controversy over the disputed territory.

Bordering the banks of the Orinoco
for many miles are the jungles and

A TROPICAL FOREST, VENEZUELA.

forests of South America, inhabited by uncivilized and aboriginal Indians. Beyond the forests spread out the *llanos* or grassy plains whereupon feed many thousand cattle of South America, which are herded by adventurous cow-boys.

To the south, midway between Bolivar and the mouth of the river, are the mining districts. The gold here discovered has given rise to the controversies between Great Britain and Venezuela over the boundary question.

XXIV.

THE DISPUTED TERRITORY.

EVER since the time when South America's wealth in gold was first reported abroad by Columbus, Raleigh, Vespucci, and others, more especially since the story of Gonzales Ximenes de Casada, the thirst for this precious mineral has brought many seekers after fortune into the wilds of South America.

Casada was an officer sent out by the Viceroy of Peru, with other officers, in charge of the expedition to search for the El Dorado of the Orinoco. He was a treacherous man of mean character. After engaging a few of the party to mutiny with him, he stole away from camp one night and with the

AMONG THE BAMBOOS, VENEZUELA.

canoes and ammunition of the expedition floated down the Orinoco. Gaining the coast after many months, he made his way to Europe, where he reported himself as having found the El Dorado of which all the world was in search. He reported that the city of Manoah was literally built of gold, which story caused a great fever of excitement, not only among the general population of Europe, but also in its courts and among its noblemen.

Prior to the discovery of gold in Guiana in 1880, all efforts to find it were unsuccessful. In the 16th and 17th centuries, when the wealth of the region south of the Orinoco, in what is now known to us as the Disputed Territory was comparatively unknown and its vast resources unexplored, there was no occasion for any boundary disputes.

We hear of gold mining along the Essequibo and its tributaries a hundred years ago by the Dutch, but it amounted to little. In 1856 a deposit was discovered which caused several companies to explore ; they also were unsuccessful and the search was abandoned. Then nothing of importance was done until 1880, when a party of French laborers from French Guiana found rich deposits in the sands of the Puruni River, a branch of the Essequibo. This caused a rush from all parts of the world, and people from California, Capetown, and the continent of Europe swarmed into the territory.

From that time until the present, new discoveries have been constantly made, and some of the resources of the country brought to view, so that the question whether this territory belongs to Venezuela or Great Britain is now of serious moment. A country which can export, as the duties show, from the city of Bolivar alone, thirty-nine million dollars' worth of gold in a few years is truly of no little importance.

There are many American and English people, as well as other foreigners, living in the mining district, although the negroes do most of the hard labor in the mines, being best suited to endure the fevers of the district and the labor necessary in the severe work of mining.

The colonial authorities of the British Government have quietly occupied this territory and have been encouraged.

Great Britain usually has a gunboat floating on the lower Orinoco. Whether the river itself belongs to Great Britain or Venezuela does not seem to have been questioned, as it appears that Great Britain rather acknowledged Venezuela in this respect by requesting her, some years ago, through the British minister at Caracas, to build a lighthouse on one of the islands.

The controversy grew out of conditions that arose in 1691 when a treaty was signed between Spain and Holland stipulating that the Orinoco colonies should belong to the Spanish and the Essequibo colonies to the Dutch. This territory was practically unknown at the time. In 1814 Holland ceded to England that part of Guiana now called British Guiana.

The question hinges greatly upon the settlement between these two nations of what properly belonged in those early times to Holland and what to Spain.

Venezuela now claims the sovereignty over a territory of 36,000 square miles which Great Britain considers as belonging to her colony of Guiana.

Through the medium of the Monroe Doctrine the controversy over the Disputed Territory has been brought into prominence throughout the United States. It is a question of vital importance, not only between the contending powers, Venezuela and Great Britain, but between England and the great republic of America.   The United States, like its emblem the eagle, which extends its broad wings to protect its young from harm or disturbance, has taken the position of affording its protection to all the younger countries of the American continent.

XXV.

DREAMS OF THE FUTURE.

AMID the charms of a moonlight night, let us imagine ourselves seated on deck, quietly floating down the Orinoco. The rays of the moon reflected on the waters turn them into a stream of pure silver. The deep forests on either side respond with gentle sighs to the caressing of the evening winds. Were it not for the splashing of an alligator as he falls heavily into the water, or the weird cry of a strange bird in his upward flight, the quiet of the scene would be undisturbed.

It must have been on such a night as this, that Ursua and his generous love Inez met their untimely and tragic death

154

while floating amid love's caresses on this same river. With our thoughts thus given to the adventurous past, we yet speculate on the destiny of this beautiful land. As the smoke from my pipe curls itself into wreaths, scenes from the past and dreams of the future float before my mind. I see armed men, covered with steel, following a bold, handsome leader, a Spanish knight. Perchance it might be Ojeda, flourishing in the kind graces of Queen Isabel.

Alas! this expedition, like so many others eager in the quest of the riches of El Dorado, cared nought for the prayers and offerings of the innocent Indians, who greeted the strangers with respect, thinking them gods from the blue sky above. The minds of the invaders being accustomed to the cruelties of war, they return such treatment on the part of the Indians with butchery and crime.

The fever of adventure having taken

possession of the Continent, many knights and adventurers seek the southern land. A century has not elapsed before the banner bearing the arms of Castile and Aragon proudly floats over the land in many places.

I see enacted before me the settlement of the country with circumstances of direst cruelty, and as the scene before me alters it is but a transition from crime to crime. After the fighting against these innocent Indians rose the bitter struggles and contest of the Spanish colonists against their unprincipled and tyrannical rulers.

It would seem that the upheaving of the mighty mountains was only to show their sympathy for the colonists. The very groaning of the great Andes is echoed by the colonists under these oppressions, and, like the mountains themselves, tired of the tyrannical choking, they show forth their nature by a series of uprisings in the form of revolutions.

Some years afterwards the cool air of the Andes moderates the fever and excitement ; but it is not until the germ of a republic has been planted. I see this germ growing into a mighty tree of state, the roots of which have fastened into a pure and honorable soil. This tree of state will in time cast a shade of protection and peace over its people. This mighty tree, called Venezuela, embedded in a soil of peace and prosperity, is one of a grove of similar South American republics still being nourished in their youth. In time the roots of these trees will become grown together and intertwined, giving forth nourishment and strength to each other and producing the rich fruits of peace, happiness, civilization, and progress.

THE END.

www.ingramcontent.com/pod-product-compliance
Lightning Source LLC
Chambersburg PA
CBHW032008060726
47497CB00017B/2396